Hurry Up, Houdini!

Magic Tree House® Books

#1: DINOSAURS BEFORE DARK
#2: THE KNIGHT AT DAWN
#3: MUMMIES IN THE MORNING
#4: PIRATES PAST NOON
#5: NIGHT OF THE NINJAS
#6: AFTERNOON ON THE AMAZON
#7: SUNSET OF THE SABERTOOTH
#8: MIDNIGHT ON THE MOON
#9: DOLPHINS AT DAYBREAK
#10: GHOST TOWN AT SUNDOWN
#11: LIONS AT LUNCHTIME
#12: POLAR BEARS PAST BEDTIME
#13: VACATION UNDER THE VOLCANO
#14: DAY OF THE DRAGON KING
#15: VIKING SHIPS AT SUNRISE
#16: HOUR OF THE OLYMPICS
#17: TONIGHT ON THE *TITANIC*
#18: BUFFALO BEFORE BREAKFAST
#19: TIGERS AT TWILIGHT
#20: DINGOES AT DINNERTIME
#21: CIVIL WAR ON SUNDAY
#22: REVOLUTIONARY WAR
    ON WEDNESDAY
#23: TWISTER ON TUESDAY
#24: EARTHQUAKE IN THE
    EARLY MORNING
#25: STAGE FRIGHT ON A
    SUMMER NIGHT
#26: GOOD MORNING, GORILLAS
#27: THANKSGIVING ON THURSDAY
#28: HIGH TIDE IN HAWAII

Merlin Missions

#29: CHRISTMAS IN CAMELOT
#30: HAUNTED CASTLE ON HALLOWS EVE
#31: SUMMER OF THE SEA SERPENT
#32: WINTER OF THE ICE WIZARD
#33: CARNIVAL AT CANDLELIGHT
#34: SEASON OF THE SANDSTORMS
#35: NIGHT OF THE NEW MAGICIANS
#36: BLIZZARD OF THE BLUE MOON
#37: DRAGON OF THE RED DAWN
#38: MONDAY WITH A MAD GENIUS
#39: DARK DAY IN THE DEEP SEA
#40: EVE OF THE EMPEROR PENGUIN
#41: MOONLIGHT ON THE MAGIC FLUTE
#42: A GOOD NIGHT FOR GHOSTS

#43: LEPRECHAUN IN LATE WINTER
#44: A GHOST TALE FOR CHRISTMAS TIME
#45: A CRAZY DAY WITH COBRAS
#46: DOGS IN THE DEAD OF NIGHT
#47: ABE LINCOLN AT LAST!
#48: A PERFECT TIME FOR PANDAS
#49: STALLION BY STARLIGHT

Magic Tree House® Fact Trackers

DINOSAURS
KNIGHTS AND CASTLES
MUMMIES AND PYRAMIDS
PIRATES
RAIN FORESTS
SPACE
TITANIC
TWISTERS AND OTHER TERRIBLE STORMS
DOLPHINS AND SHARKS
ANCIENT GREECE AND THE OLYMPICS
AMERICAN REVOLUTION
SABERTOOTHS AND THE ICE AGE
PILGRIMS
ANCIENT ROME AND POMPEII
TSUNAMIS AND OTHER NATURAL DISASTERS
POLAR BEARS AND THE ARCTIC
SEA MONSTERS
PENGUINS AND ANTARCTICA
LEONARDO DA VINCI
GHOSTS
LEPRECHAUNS AND IRISH FOLKLORE
RAGS AND RICHES: KIDS IN THE TIME OF
    CHARLES DICKENS
SNAKES AND OTHER REPTILES
DOG HEROES
ABRAHAM LINCOLN
PANDAS AND OTHER ENDANGERED SPECIES
HORSE HEROES

More Magic Tree House®

GAMES AND PUZZLES FROM THE TREE HOUSE

MAGIC TRICKS FROM THE TREE HOUSE

MAGIC TREE HOUSE® #50
A MERLIN MISSION

Hurry Up, Houdini!

by Mary Pope Osborne

illustrated by Sal Murdocca

A STEPPING STONE BOOK™
Random House 🏠 New York

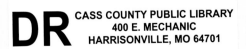

For the Korner family,
Jim, Toni, Courtney, and Tom

Text copyright © 2013 by Mary Pope Osborne
Jacket art and interior illustrations copyright © 2013 by Sal Murdocca

All rights reserved. Published in the United States by Random House Children's Books, a division of Random House, Inc., New York.

Random House and the colophon are registered trademarks and A Stepping Stone Book and the colophon are trademarks of Random House, Inc. Magic Tree House is a registered trademark of Mary Pope Osborne; used under license.

Visit us on the Web!
randomhouse.com/kids
MagicTreeHouse.com

Educators and librarians, for a variety of teaching tools, visit us at
RHTeachersLibrarians.com

Library of Congress Cataloging-in-Publication Data
Osborne, Mary Pope.
Hurry up, Houdini! / by Mary Pope Osborne ; illustrated by Sal Murdocca.
  p. cm. — (Magic tree house ; #50)
Summary: "Join Jack and Annie as they meet one of the world's most famous illusionists—Harry Houdini!" —Provided by publisher.
ISBN 978-0-307-98045-8 (trade) — ISBN 978-0-307-98046-5 (lib. bdg.) —
ISBN 978-0-307-98047-2 (ebook)
[1. Time travel—Fiction. 2. Magicians—Fiction. 3. Houdini, Harry, 1874–1926—Fiction.
4. New York (N.Y.)—History—20th century—Fiction. 5. Magic—Fiction.
6. Tree houses—Fiction.] I. Murdocca, Sal, illustrator. II. Title.
PZ7.O81167Hur 2013   [Fic]—dc23   2012045610

Printed in the United States of America
10 9 8 7 6 5 4 3 2 1

CONTENTS

Prologue

One summer day in Frog Creek, Pennsylvania, a mysterious tree house appeared in the woods. It was filled with books. A boy named Jack and his sister, Annie, found the tree house and soon discovered that it was magic. They could go to any time and place in history just by pointing to a picture in one of the books. While they were gone, no time at all passed back in Frog Creek.

Jack and Annie eventually found out that the tree house belonged to Morgan le Fay, a magical librarian from the legendary realm of Camelot. They have since traveled on many adventures in the magic tree house and completed many missions for both Morgan le Fay and her friend Merlin the magician.

Now Merlin needs Jack and Annie's help again. He wants them to travel through time and learn secrets of greatness from four people who are called great by the world. Jack and Annie have just returned from the first of these four missions: a trip to ancient Macedonia, where they spent time with Alexander the Great and his warhorse, Bucephalus.

Back in Frog Creek, they are waiting to find out where Merlin will send them to find the next secret of greatness. . . .

CHAPTER ONE

Message from Merlin

Early one summer evening, Jack lay on the couch, reading a book about the history of horses.

"Jack, could you run and get Annie from Jenny's house, please?" their mom called from the kitchen. "We're grilling hot dogs soon."

"Sure," said Jack. He closed his book, hopped off the couch, and headed out the front door. As he started down the porch steps, Annie charged into the yard.

"It's back!" she said, out of breath.

"You're kidding!" said Jack.

"No! I'm serious!" said Annie. "On my way home from Jenny's, I checked the woods. I had a funny feeling it was back—and it was!"

"Are Merlin and Penny there?" asked Jack.

"I don't think so," said Annie. "I shouted hello, but no one answered. I wanted to come get you before I climbed up!"

"Thanks," said Jack. "Wait here. I'll tell Mom." He dashed back into the house. "Mom, can Annie and I do something for about twenty minutes?" he called.

"Okay, twenty minutes, no more," said their mom. "The grill's almost ready."

"Thanks!" said Jack. He looked at his wristwatch. It was 5:42. So they had to be home by two minutes after six. He grabbed his backpack and hurried out of the house. Annie was waiting on the sidewalk.

"Twenty minutes! No more!" Jack called, running toward her.

"No problem!" Annie said, and they hurried up the sidewalk together.

"I'll bet Merlin wants us to find another secret of greatness," said Jack.

"I know," said Annie. "I can't wait!"

They crossed the street and headed into the Frog Creek woods. They ran through the shadowy light until they came to the tallest oak.

"Merlin? Penny?" Annie called.

There was no answer. The woods were still, strangely still. Not a leaf moved.

"Let's go up," said Jack. He grabbed the rope ladder and started climbing. Annie followed. When they scrambled into the tree house, there was no sign of Merlin or Penny.

"Not here," said Annie.

"Nope," said Jack. "But everything else is."

He pointed to a piece of paper lying on the floor in the corner. On the paper he'd written the secret of greatness they'd learned on their last mission:

HUMILITY

Sitting on top of the paper were two things—

a small gold ring and a tiny bottle. Annie picked up the ring and held it out to Jack. "The Ring of Truth," she said. "You get to wear it this time."

"Thanks," said Jack. He took the gold ring and slipped it onto his finger.

"Just make sure you keep checking to see if it's glowing," said Annie.

"Don't worry, I will," said Jack. According to

Merlin, the Ring of Truth would glow only when Jack and Annie discovered a true secret of greatness.

Annie picked up the tiny bottle. She and Jack stared at its swirling contents. "Wow," she breathed. "Merlin's magic mist."

Jack repeated the words of Camelot's magician: "Mist gathered at first light on the first day of the new moon on the Isle of Avalon."

"Good memory," said Annie.

"Who wouldn't remember *that*?" said Jack. "If we take a sniff, we can be great at anything we choose for one hour."

"That's so cool," said Annie.

"Yeah," said Jack. He had loved becoming a great horse trainer on their last mission. "I wonder what talent we'll have this time. And where will we go?"

Annie pointed at a booklet that was lying in the shadows. She picked it up and handed it to Jack.

"Coney Island, I think," she said.

Jack read the title:

"Coney Island. Isn't that in New York?" said Annie.

"Yep. Look, there's a note inside," said Jack. He pulled out a piece of parchment from the booklet. He read aloud:

Dear Jack and Annie,
Thank you for successfully completing your first mission to find a secret of greatness. Now on your new mission, I would like you to learn a second secret— this time, from the Great Houdini.

—M.

"Oh, man, the Great Houdini!" said Jack.

"What did he do?" said Annie.

"Dad told me about him," said Jack. "He could escape from anything! Chains, ropes, locks, handcuffs, prisons. He was amazing!"

"Was he a criminal?" said Annie.

Jack laughed. "No, he was a performer—the greatest escape artist who ever lived," he said. "He performed his act all over the world. I can't believe we're actually going to meet him!"

"So where do we find a person like that?" asked Annie.

"Coney Island!" said Jack, holding up the booklet.

"Oh, yeah, duh," said Annie. "So make the wish and let's go!"

"Okay!" said Jack. He put Merlin's message and the magic mist into his backpack. Then he pointed to the words *Coney Island* on the booklet. "I wish we could go there!"

The wind started to blow.

The tree house started to spin.

It spun faster and faster.

Then everything was still.

Absolutely still.

CHAPTER TWO

My Treat!

Jack heard people laughing and shouting. A brass band was playing a lively tune. He and Annie looked out the window. The tree house had landed in a cluster of trees. High above the trees were towers, turrets, domes, and spires.

"Are those castles?" asked Annie. "Did we land in the Middle Ages?"

"Definitely not," said Jack. "Look at our clothes." In the dim light inside the tree house, Jack could see that he was wearing knee-length pants, a long-sleeved shirt, high socks, and lace-up boots. His backpack was now a leather bag.

"You're right," said Annie. She was wearing a sailor dress and a pair of boots. "These are like the clothes we wore when we went to San Francisco."

"Yep, in the early 1900s," said Jack. He reached into one of his pockets and took out a watch on a chain. "Look, I have a pocket watch now instead of a wristwatch. And"—from the other pocket, Jack pulled out a handful of coins—"a bunch of pennies!"

"Just pennies? That's all?" said Annie.

"Don't worry," said Jack. "I once read that a penny in 1900 was worth the same as a quarter in our time."

"Cool, we're rich," said Annie with a laugh.

"Here, take some," said Jack. He gave Annie half of his handful of coins.

"Thanks," Annie said, dropping the pennies into the pocket of her dress. "Okay! Let's find out what's going on here!" She headed down the ladder. Jack slung his bag over his shoulder and followed her.

Jack and Annie stepped down into a walled garden lit by a string of tiny lights. They walked together down a pebbled path and over a small bridge that crossed a brook. Then they came to a wooden gate with a sign that said THANKS FOR VISITING THE JAPANESE TEA GARDEN.

"We landed in a Japanese tea garden?" said Jack. "What's that about?"

"Keep going," said Annie. She opened the gate, and they stepped from the shadowy garden into a bright open space.

"Wow!" they said together.

Beneath the turrets and towers, thousands of electric lights lit up the evening sky. A big band played on a raised platform near a lake. Men in white suits and women in long white dresses strolled down a broad avenue. Children dressed like Jack and Annie darted about, shouting and pointing at different attractions:

A TRIP TO THE MOON

MOUNTAIN TORRENT

KANSAS CYCLONE

The air smelled of salt water, roasting nuts, and popcorn. Vendors shouted: "Step right up! World's greatest ice cream! Strawberry! Vanilla!" "World's greatest pink lemonade!" "World's greatest hot dogs!"

"What *is* this place?" said Annie.

Jack opened their booklet and read:

Located in southern Brooklyn, in New York City, Coney Island is actually a peninsula—a piece of land *nearly* surrounded by water. Coney Island is world-famous for its dazzling amusement parks.

"Of course, I understand," said Jack. "We landed in an amusement park."

"I love it!" said Annie. "Let's get a hot dog!"

"No, we'd better not," said Jack. "We should find Houdini first. Let's see if the guidebook says anything about him." He opened their booklet and thumbed through the pages. "Houdini . . . Houdini . . ." He ran his finger down a page. "Hey, here's an ad for his show!"

Jack read aloud:

DON'T MISS
the
Great Houdini!
HENDERSON'S
‹**MUSIC HALL**›
SURF AVENUE
JUNE 22, 1908 9:00 PM

"Oh, wow," said Annie. "Our tourist booklet must be from 1908! And I bet Merlin wants us to see Houdini at Henderson's Music Hall! Excuse me," she called to a couple strolling by. "Is today by any chance June twenty-second, 1908?"

The woman laughed. "It is indeed," she said.

"Thanks!" said Annie.

Jack pulled out his pocket watch. "It's six-forty right now," he said.

"Oh, we have *tons* of time," said Annie. "C'mon. Let's get a hot dog."

"No," said Jack, "I think we should get our tickets. They might—"

"We have over two hours!" Annie interrupted. "It doesn't take long to eat a hot dog. My treat!" She grabbed Jack and pulled him toward the hot dog stand.

"Okay, okay," Jack said, sighing. Actually the smells coming from the stand were pretty wonderful.

"How much?" Annie said to a girl grilling hot dogs on a portable stove.

"Three cents each," the girl answered, "or two for a nickel."

"No problem! Two, please!" said Annie. She counted out five pennies and gave them to the girl.

The girl wrapped two hot dogs in white bread

and loaded them with relish. She passed them to Annie and Jack.

Jack took a giant bite. "Hmm—dewicious!" he said with his mouth full. "Iz gweatest wha dawg eh de wawld."

Annie nodded. "Wewy gweatest!" she said, her mouth full, too.

When they finished eating, they wiped their mouths with a handkerchief from Jack's pocket. "Okay! Let's get our Houdini tickets now!" he said.

"Wait, we still have time for ice cream," said Annie. "They have strawberry. Your favorite!"

"Hmm . . . ice cream?" said Jack.

"It'll just take two minutes," said Annie. "The greatest in the world, remember?"

"Okay, *my* treat," said Jack.

"Yay. Thanks!" said Annie.

They hurried to the window of a small ice cream shop. "Two cones of strawberry," Jack said.

"Four cents," the ice cream man said.

Jack handed over four pennies. The man scooped strawberry ice cream into two sweet-smelling waffle cones and handed them to Jack. Jack and Annie ate their ice cream as they strolled up the dazzling avenue, passing different rides and attractions.

"Trip to the Moon!" a young man shouted at them. "Get your tickets here!"

"Been there!" Jack said.

"Done that," added Annie.

A boy in a fur parka rolled by on a unicycle. "Tickets for a submarine ride!" he yelled to Jack and Annie. "Departing soon for the North Pole!"

"Been there!" said Annie.

"Done that," said Jack.

"Kansas Cyclone!" a girl shouted from the entrance of a large tent. "Come inside and be blown away!"

"Been there. Done that, too," said Jack.

Annie laughed.

As soon as he finished his ice cream cone, Jack wiped his hands and opened their booklet. "Okay. Now we have to get serious," he said. "I wonder where Surf Avenue is."

"Hey, I see something we haven't done before," said Annie. "Look!"

Annie pointed to a boat filled with screaming passengers splashing down a tall, watery slide. The boat crashed into a lake and shot under an arched bridge. The riders shrieked as they bounced up into the air. Then the boat glided across the lake to a landing.

"Shoot-the-Chutes!" a man yelled from a ticket booth. "Only one dime! Jump aboard!"

"Wow, that looks like so much fun! Let's do it. My treat," said Annie. Before Jack could say anything, she dashed to the booth.

Jack quickly followed her. "No, Annie," he said. "I want to get our tickets for the Houdini show *now*."

But Annie had already pulled out a bunch of pennies and was paying for two tickets.

"I said I didn't—" Jack said.

"Oh, please!" Annie said, handing Jack his ticket. "We have plenty of time. One little ride won't hurt us."

Jack sighed. "But I—" he started.

"Come on, come on," Annie said. "We'll get Houdini tickets right after this, I promise. This will just take an extra five minutes, that's all."

"Okay, you win," said Jack. "Let's go."

Jack followed Annie to a boat. The last passengers were climbing out, talking and laughing. Others were waiting to climb in—four giggling teenage girls and a short man and woman who both wore large hats. The woman's hat was piled high with fake roses and bananas.

"The kids ride up front!" the boatman said.

Jack and Annie stepped into the boat, and the teenagers and the couple in the hats took seats behind them. The boatman sat in the back. Soon cables began pulling the boat up a ramp that led to the top of the slide.

"Whoa," Jack breathed as the boat climbed higher and higher. The amusement park shimmered below. Hundreds of flags flapped from turrets and towers.

What keeps the boat from tumbling off its

tracks? Jack wondered. "There're no seat belts here," he grumbled to Annie, "or safety bars, or anything. How do people keep from falling out of this thing?"

"I don't know," said Annie, sighing. "But could you just try to have fun? It's a normal, everyday ride."

"Yeah, well, we don't really have time for a normal, everyday ride," said Jack. "We should have gotten our tickets for the Houdini show already."

"You don't have to be so grouchy," said Annie.

"I'm not grouchy," Jack said grouchily. "But why do we always do what you want to do?"

Before Annie could answer, the boat swiveled on a turnaround at the top of the ramp. Then it jerked forward and barreled down the slide toward the lake!

"AHHHHHH!" Jack yelled.

CHAPTER THREE

S-O-L-D O-U-T

The boat splashed into the lake and shot under the arched bridge. Then it bounced into the air, splashing water everywhere. Jack closed his eyes and ducked his head. All the teenagers screamed. For a moment the boat seemed to fly! Then it landed back on the lake and steadied itself.

Jack opened his eyes and looked around.

Annie was laughing with the other passengers as the boat glided peacefully across the water. Everyone seemed to be having fun. But Jack's heart was thumping and his stomach felt queasy.

The boatman docked the boat and helped everyone onto the landing. The passengers scattered in different directions.

"Okay! Time to go to the theater!" said Annie.

"Wait, I need to sit for a minute," said Jack.

"I thought you were desperate to get our tickets," said Annie.

"In a minute," said Jack. He pointed to a terrace that bordered the lake. "How about we sit over there?"

"Sure," Annie said. "Are you okay?"

"I will be," said Jack. "Come on."

Jack and Annie climbed a couple of steps to the terrace and sat at the end of a crowded bench. All around them, people in costumes were hawking tickets to different rides.

"Step this way, ladies and gentlemen! Enter the Dragon's Gorge! Greatest roller coaster in the country!" shouted a man wearing a dragon head.

"Over here! The Buzzard's Roost!" called a boy in a bird outfit. "Greatest train ride on earth!"

"Come to the Babbling Brook!" yelled a girl

dressed as a mermaid. "Greatest water ride in the U.S. of A.!"

"Funny. Sounds like *everything* in Coney Island is the greatest," said Jack.

"So?" said Annie.

"That means *nothing's* really the greatest," said Jack, "because everything's the same!"

"Ha!" A woman sitting on the bench laughed.

Jack realized they were sitting next to the short couple from the Shoot-the-Chutes ride. Their big hats almost completely hid their faces.

"Did you hear that, Harry?" the woman said to the man. "This boy's a genius!"

"Ain't that the truth, Bess?" Harry said.

"Don't say *ain't*, dear. Say *isn't*," Bess said kindly.

Harry smiled at Jack and Annie. "*Isn't* that the truth?" he said. "See, my Bess is always looking after me."

Jack and Annie smiled politely.

"Is this your first time in Coney Island, kiddos?" asked Harry.

"It is," said Annie. "Yours, too?"

"Oh, no!" said Bess. "No, no, no. We first met here at Coney Island fifteen years ago. We got married three weeks later!"

"Congratulations," said Annie.

"It was a long time ago," said Bess. "But I'm more crazy about him than ever. And he writes me a love note every day, rain or shine."

"That's so sweet," said Annie.

"Are you kiddos having a good time here?" asked Harry.

"*I* am," said Annie.

"Good," said Bess. Then she turned to her husband. "Time's running out, dreamboat," she said. "We'd better move on."

"Can we get ice cream cones now?" Harry asked.

"No! You know the routine—ice cream always comes *after* the show!" Bess said. "If we want to take the Trip to the Moon, we gotta go now."

Harry looked at Jack and Annie. "She's always wanted to send me to the moon," he said.

Jack and Annie laughed.

"You kiddos want to join us?" Harry asked.

"I'm sorry, we can't," said Jack. "We have to do something else. Hey, do you know where Henderson's Music Hall is?"

"Sure. Why do you want to know?" Bess asked.

"We're going to see the Great Houdini," said Jack.

"Ah! What a coincidence!" said Bess. "We're going there, too, after our Trip to the Moon. I adore that man—the Great Houdini! I wouldn't miss watching *that* dreamboat for anything in this world."

Harry cleared his throat. "Sweetheart, they want directions," he said.

"Oh, yes!" said Bess. "So, walk the main road there to the arches, and then exit the park." She pointed to giant gold-colored arches in the distance. "Then turn right and head down Surf Avenue. When you see a big red building, stop. That's it."

"Cool," said Jack. "Thanks."

"So long, kiddos. Maybe we'll see you later at the Great Houdini show," said Harry.

"And when you watch the show, remember," said Bess, "even though everything can't be the greatest, sometimes what folks call great really *is* great."

Harry laughed. He tipped his straw hat to Jack and Annie, and he and Bess walked away.

"I liked them," said Annie.

"Me too," said Jack. He stood up. Talking with the cheerful couple had made him feel better. "Okay! Let's go get our tickets! Finally!"

Jack and Annie stepped down from the terrace and walked up the broad avenue toward the arches. At the arches, they passed ticket sellers sitting in red chariots. "Hurry back to Luna Park!" one shouted.

"We will, don't worry!" said Annie.

Jack and Annie left Luna Park and stepped onto Surf Avenue. "Bess said to go right," said Jack.

As Jack and Annie started up the crowded

sidewalk, they passed horses and buggies and old-timey cars. The warm summer night was filled with the sounds of hooves clomping and horns honking: *Ah-OO-ga! Ah-OO-ga!*

"There it is!" said Jack. He pointed to a large red building with green trim. A big sign over the awning read HENDERSON'S.

A huge crowd of people had lined up on the sidewalk in front of the theater. "Oh, man, look at that line!" said Jack. "This is why I wanted to be here *early*!"

Jack and Annie ran to the end of the line, where some teenagers were joking and pushing each other around.

"Is this the line to buy tickets?" asked Annie.

"Nah, this is for folks who got theirs already. Like us!" said a tough-looking kid. "So scram!"

"Forget it," said Jack. He pulled Annie along. "We have to find the box office."

At the front of the theater was a chalkboard that read:

MAGIC TONIGHT!

8:15: The Bambini Brothers
9:00: The Great Houdini

◄ **TICKETS HERE!** ►

Jack hurried to a window beside the chalkboard. He was surprised there was no line. "Excuse me!" he said, trying to get the attention of the ticket seller. She was talking to a man inside the office.

"You're not listening to me, Mrs. Crenshaw!" the man shouted. "It *is* the end of the world! I tell you, they'll destroy the theater!"

"Excuse me!" Jack said again, in a louder voice. "We'd like to buy two—"

"They'll start a riot! They'll tear the seats apart!" the man shouted. "Mercy! Mercy, my heart!" He clutched his chest and nearly collapsed.

"Should we get help?" Annie asked.

Mrs. Crenshaw looked down at Annie and shook her head. "No, dear. Mr. Dewey will be fine," she said. She rolled her eyes.

"Yes! Get help! Get help, please!" Mr. Dewey croaked, wiping his brow with a handkerchief. "Find me a new opening act!"

"A what?" said Annie.

"The Bambini Brothers ran off!" said Mr. Dewey. "I caught them red-handed! Stealing from the box office!"

"That sounds terrible," said Annie.

"You have no idea, missy!" cried Mr. Dewey. "They were the opening act for the Great Houdini!"

He wiped his sweaty face again. "The hooligans in the crowd will go crazy if the curtain's late! I should have gone into the *shoe* business instead of show business!"

Jack felt sorry for the man, but he really didn't care about the Bambini Brothers. He just wanted tickets for the Great Houdini. "Uh . . . excuse me," he said to Mrs. Crenshaw. "We'd like to buy two tickets for the big show—the one with the Great Houdini."

"Sorry, kids, didn't you read that?" Mrs. Crenshaw said. She pointed to a sign in the window. The sign read: SOLD OUT.

"Oh, no, we didn't see that," said Annie.

"You're . . . sold out?" said Jack.

"Yes!" yelled Mr. Dewey. "We sold out an hour ago! S-O-L-D O-U-T! So it's a full house with no opening act! Go away now, please! We got problems! Big problems!" And with that, Mr. Dewey slammed the box office window shut.

CHAPTER FOUR

Okay! Good-Bye!

"Sold out," Jack said to Annie, "an hour ago."

"I know. You were right. I was wrong," Annie said quickly. "We *should* have come earlier."

Jack just stared at her.

"I'm sorry," said Annie, making a face. "Really." She looked around. "So, do you think anyone in line would sell us *their* tickets?"

"Not in a million years," said Jack. "I can't believe this. How can we meet Houdini now? And learn his secret of greatness?"

"We'll figure something out," said Annie. "We

always do. Don't worry. Let's think. . . ." She pulled on her braids and bit her lip as she stared at the window of the box office.

Jack couldn't get over his frustration. "I—I just can't believe it," he said. "Maybe *this* is the secret of greatness: *Don't listen to your sister! Buy your tickets ahead of time!*" He held up his hand and wiggled his finger. "Afraid the Ring of Truth isn't glowing," he said. "Too bad."

"Wait a minute!" said Annie. "Doesn't this remind you of the time we went to Shakespeare's theater in London and the two actors didn't show up for the play?"

"I don't want to talk about our other missions now," Jack said. He pulled out their booklet and turned the pages, hoping to find more information about Houdini.

"But don't you remember how Shakespeare put you and me in the play instead?" said Annie.

Jack ignored her. "I don't see anything else in here about Houdini . . . just this one show," he said, scanning each page.

"It was so cool! And we had a great time. Do you want to give it a try?" said Annie. "Do you?"

Jack closed the booklet. "Do I *what*?" he asked.

"Do you want to use Merlin's magic mist and make a wish to be great stage magicians?" said Annie.

"Stage magicians?" said Jack.

"Yes! *You and me!* We go onstage in place of the Bambini Brothers!" said Annie.

"What? Are you out of your mind?" said Jack.

"Think about it! It's a great plan! That way, we can meet Houdini backstage! We'll be fellow performers!" said Annie. "Plus we'll be helping out Mr. Dewey and his theater! And, not to mention, it would be incredibly fun!"

"That plan's ridiculous," said Jack. "No one's going to let us go onstage and do a magic show."

"You are so wrong. I'll bet I can make it happen," said Annie. "Watch."

"Wait!" said Jack.

But Annie dashed to the box office window and tapped on the glass. When Mrs. Crenshaw opened the window, Annie leaned forward and spoke in a hushed voice.

"What are you saying to her?" Jack called.

Mrs. Crenshaw immediately closed the window and left the box office.

"Annie, what did you say?" asked Jack.

The theater door swung open. "Inside! Quick!" Mrs. Crenshaw said to Annie.

"Wait! Where are you going?" Jack started to follow Annie into the theater, but the door closed behind her and locked.

Jack went back to the box office and looked through the window. Annie was talking enthusiastically to Mrs. Crenshaw and Mr. Dewey. Jack couldn't hear a word she was saying.

Jack tapped on the window and shook his head, but Annie ignored him. As she kept talking, Mr. Dewey's expressions changed from frowning to squinting to smiling to laughing, until suddenly he shouted, "Yes!"

No! thought Jack.

With a big grin, Annie shot her fist into the air.

The next thing Jack knew, she was racing out of the theater door. "I did it! I did it! We have a show to do!" she cried. "He said yes!"

"But *I* didn't say yes!" said Jack.

"Don't worry! I fixed everything—for us and Mr. Dewey!" said Annie.

"What did you tell him?" said Jack.

Before Annie could answer, Mr. Dewey rushed out of the theater. "Hurry, kids!" he shouted.

"Come on!" Annie grabbed Jack's hand and pulled him toward the door.

Mr. Dewey pushed Jack and Annie into the theater and locked the door behind them. "George!" he called to an usher. "Quick, change the sign! Erase the Bambinis! Write 'Jolly Jack and the Amazing Annie' instead!"

Jolly Jack? thought Jack.

"This way!" Mr. Dewey hustled Jack and Annie through the theater lobby and into a large auditorium. The auditorium had rows and rows of floor seats, as well as box seats and a balcony. Electric lights cast a peach-colored glow over a stage framed by a red curtain.

"Is that where we'll perform?" Annie asked.

"No way! No way!" Jack whispered to her.

"Yes! That very stage!" boomed Mr. Dewey.

In the orchestra pit, a violinist was making squeaky sounds, a drummer was setting up his cymbals, and a trumpet player was practicing on his horn.

"Do they play tonight?" said Annie.

"For the Houdini show," said Mr. Dewey. "But if you like, I'm sure they can accompany your routine, too."

"Yes! I like!" said Annie. She turned to Jack. "Did you hear that? We get music!"

"Annie, I didn't agree to do this," Jack said under his breath. He was fuming.

"Come along to your dressing room," said Mr. Dewey.

Jack didn't move. But Annie skipped down the aisle after Mr. Dewey.

"I didn't agree, Annie!" Jack yelled from the back of the auditorium. The clashing cymbals drowned out his voice. "Annie, come back!" he yelled louder.

But Annie followed Mr. Dewey through a door to the backstage area.

"Darn her!" said Jack, and he hurried down the aisle. He slipped through the door marked BACKSTAGE and stepped into an empty hallway.

"Where did she go?" Jack muttered. He heard voices. He walked down the hall to the backstage area, where he found Mr. Dewey talking to a bald man with a clipboard.

"There he is!" said Annie, pointing at Jack.

"Meet Jolly Jack!" Mr. Dewey said to the bald man. "Other half of the famous brother-and-sister team Jolly Jack and the Amazing Annie!"

"These little kids are filling in for the Bambinis tonight?" the bald man asked.

"We're not so little," said Annie, "and we've been stage magicians for years."

"Excuse me. My sister's made a mistake. We can't do this," said Jack. "We . . . we don't have our costumes. We don't have *anything*!"

"Not a problem," said Mr. Dewey. "The Bambinis left all their props and costumes behind."

"See?" Annie said to Jack.

"But—" started Jack.

"I'm turning you over to Mr. Wilson, our stage manager, now," said Mr. Dewey. "Good luck! I have to tell Mrs. Crenshaw to open the doors and let the hordes inside. The show will go on!" Mr. Dewey then disappeared down the hall.

"You kids better know what you're doing," said Mr. Wilson, shaking his head. "Saturday-night crowds can be pretty wild."

"Don't worry," Annie said with a grin. "Our magic act can get pretty wild, too."

Jack couldn't believe her! She had completely taken over their whole mission!

Mr. Wilson laughed. "Good," he said. "I'm glad you're so confident, Amazing Annie. Come with me. Your dressing room is next to Mr. Houdini's."

"Cool! Is Mr. Houdini here now?" Annie asked as they followed Mr. Wilson.

"Nope, he won't get here before eight-thirty," said Mr. Wilson. He led them down the hallway and opened a door.

"Here you go." The stage manager waved Jack and Annie into a small room. "See, the Bambinis left behind all their stuff. Use anything you need. You can wear their costumes, too. Both guys were kind of short."

"It all looks great," said Annie.

On the dressing table were wands, cards, silver

rings the size of dinner plates, top hats, bow ties, and white gloves. Strewn over a chair were tuxedos, shirts, and vests.

"Oh, wow. Look!" said Annie.

On the floor were two cages. One held three white rabbits. The other held two white doves.

"They're so cute!" said Annie. "What are they doing here?"

"They're part of the act," said Mr. Wilson. He looked puzzled. "Most magicians use doves and rabbits. You don't?"

"Oh, sure," Annie said quickly. "Absolutely, we do."

"This is crazy," said Jack. "We can't just use the Bambinis' animals and birds and costumes and props. What—what if they come back?"

"They won't be back," said Mr. Wilson. "Dewey's threatened to call the police. They've stolen from the theater twice now. After the show, Mrs. Crenshaw's going to take the birds and rabbits home to her kids."

"Oh, nice!" said Annie.

"You have thirty-five minutes," said Mr. Wilson, looking at his pocket watch. "You'll go on at fifteen minutes after eight and do a thirty-minute show. Got it?"

"Okey dokey!" said Annie.

"Good. Get ready! I'll call for you!" said Mr. Wilson. The stage manager left, closing the door.

Annie grinned at Jack. "Do you believe this?" she said.

"No. I. Don't," Jack said coldly.

The smile left Annie's face. "What's wrong? You don't seem very jolly," she said.

"I'm *not* jolly," Jack said. "I'm angry. *Really* angry."

"Why?" asked Annie.

"Because we didn't decide on this together," said Jack. "You didn't even listen to me. Just like you didn't listen to me when I wanted to buy our tickets early."

"But with the magic mist, this could be so much fun, don't you think?" said Annie. "Plus we'll meet the Great Houdini for sure. And—and we'll help

Mr. Dewey and his theater. It's a good plan, Jack!"

"It might be a good plan," said Jack. "That's not the point. The point is we didn't talk about it together. We're supposed to be a team on our missions."

"But if it's a good plan, what difference does it make if we didn't talk about it?" said Annie. "Why can't you just go along with me?"

"Because I don't want to," said Jack. "*You* decided by yourself to do this—so just do it by yourself. Just go on the stage and use the magic mist all by yourself."

"Really?" said Annie.

"Really!" said Jack.

"Well, fine," said Annie.

"Okay, then," said Jack.

"Good-bye," said Annie.

"Good-bye!" said Jack. He stormed out of the dressing room, banging the door shut behind him. He walked briskly down the backstage hallway, through the doors, and into the auditorium.

A rowdy crowd was streaming down the aisles.

Ushers yelled at teenagers who were shoving each other and fighting over their seats. *Hooligans,* Jack thought, glad he didn't have to perform.

Jack made his way through the auditorium, then through the packed lobby. He slipped by the ticket taker and squeezed past people streaming into the theater.

Jack walked away from Henderson's Music Hall as fast as he could. He hurried up the avenue, weaving his way through the crowds on the sidewalk.

She can just do it by herself, Jack thought. *I don't care. She can use Merlin's magic mist all by herself! She can perform for the hooligans and the hordes if she wants to! But I don't have to! She can sniff the magic mist and just . . . oh. OH!*

Jack stopped. He dug into his brown bag. He pulled out the small bottle. "Oh, no," he moaned. Annie didn't have Merlin's magic mist. *He* did!

CHAPTER FIVE

Together

Jack whirled around and started back up Surf Avenue. The sidewalk was so crowded, he had to jump off the curb into the street and trot alongside the old-timey cars and the horses and buggies.

When Jack reached the theater, people were still making their way inside. He squeezed through the crowd, trying not to push anyone too hard. "Excuse me, excuse me," he said. He tried to sneak his way past the ticket taker, but the man grabbed him. "Ticket, sonny?"

"I don't have a ticket," said Jack. "I just need to get backstage fast."

"Beat it, kid," said the ticket taker.

"Wait!" said Jack. He pointed at the chalkboard announcing their act. "I'm Jolly Jack. See?"

"I don't see nothing jolly about you!" said the ticket seller. "Beat it now or I'll call the cops. Next!"

Jack backed away from the door. He pulled out his pocket watch. It was ten minutes to eight! Annie had to go on at eight-fifteen! He paced up and down the sidewalk, desperately looking for another entrance.

There must be a door somewhere that leads backstage! he thought. He peered down a long, narrow alley beside the theater. The alley was dark, except for the glow of light from high windows above a row of garbage cans.

Jack hurried down the alley. A rat skittered out from behind a can. Jack kept going until he rounded the corner. He found the back entrance, but when he tried the handle, it was locked. He banged and banged on the door, but no one answered.

The windows! Jack thought. He hurried back into the alley. To reach the row of windows, he had to step from a packing crate onto the top of a garbage can. Jack stood on his toes and looked through a lit window. He saw a hallway, but no one was there. He carefully stepped from one garbage can to another until he reached the next window.

Jack looked through the glass into the Bambinis' dressing room. He saw Annie dressed in an oversized tuxedo. She was staring at a piece of paper.

Jack pounded on the window. "Annie! Annie!" he shouted, panting.

When Annie saw him, her face lit up. "Hi!" she yelled. She put down the paper and jumped onto a chair. She lifted a latch and then pushed the window up. "Thanks for coming back!" she cried. "I am so sorry, Jack!"

"Don't worry about it," he said.

"Are you coming in?" asked Annie.

"Yeah. Hold on." Jack jumped down and picked up the packing crate. He placed it on top of the garbage can. Then he carefully climbed onto the can and the crate. Clutching the windowsill, he hoisted himself through the window.

Annie helped him step down onto a chair, and then onto the floor.

Jack reached into his bag and pulled out the small bottle. "You'll need this before you go . . . onstage," he said, out of breath. "Mist gathered at first light . . . on the first day . . . of the new moon . . . on the Isle of Avalon."

"Thanks!" said Annie, taking the bottle. "When I realized I didn't have it, I didn't know what to do."

"That's what I figured," said Jack.

Annie grabbed the paper from the table. "Look at this," she said, handing it to Jack. "The Bambini Brothers must have left it."

Jack and Annie looked at the paper together. "It looks like a list of tricks," said Jack. He read:

Instant Wand
Three Bunnies
Miracle Doves
Cards from Thin Air
Chinese Rings

"Yeah, I think I have all the props for them," said Annie. "See? There are two wands, three rabbits, two doves, a pack of cards, and three big rings."

"Yeah, it's all here . . . ," said Jack.

"But what do I do with it?" said Annie.

"Maybe you'll find out when you use the magic mist," said Jack.

"Oh, yes, I bet I will!" said Annie.

"Yeah," Jack said.

"Now I can't wait to find out what's going to happen!" said Annie.

"Bet you'll have a good time," said Jack.

"What are you thinking?" asked Annie. "Should I still perform all by myself? Or do you think maybe we should perform *together*?"

Jack stared at her a moment, then sighed. "Together," he said softly.

"Yay!" said Annie. "We'll be a great team. I promise." She held up the bottle. "Should we use this right *now*? Do you want to?"

"Hmm," said Jack. "Yeah. Then we'll be able to figure everything out. But remember, the magic only works for one hour." He looked at his watch. "It's five after eight. If we start the magic now, we'll be great stage magicians until five after nine."

"No problem!" said Annie. "We go on at eight-fifteen for thirty minutes. That means we'll leave the stage at eight-forty-five."

There was a knock on the door. Mr. Wilson poked his head inside, and the noise of the audience rushed into the room like a lion's roar. Jack heard stamping and whistling and shouting.

"You go on in ten minutes!" Mr. Wilson said.

"Thanks," said Annie.

The door closed. Jack looked at Annie in a panic. "Did you hear that crowd?" he said.

"Don't think about it," said Annie. "Quick, let's use the magic!" She pulled the cork out of the bottle. "Ready?"

Jack nodded.

Annie held the bottle under her nose. "We wish to be two *great* stage magicians!" she said, and she took a deep breath. "Ahhh!" Then she handed the bottle to Jack.

Jack closed his eyes and inhaled the mist. It smelled of dewy grass, sparkling lake water, and wild thyme. He stuck the cork back into the bottle and put the bottle into the pocket of his pants.

Jack gave Annie a big grin. He felt like a new person. The crowd wasn't scary anymore. In fact, he could hardly wait to get on the stage and show them what he could do.

"Okay!" Jack said, clapping his hands. "I'd better put on my costume!" He grabbed the extra tuxedo and slipped behind a dressing curtain.

As he changed his clothes, Jack realized that everything was slightly too big. But it didn't bother him. Not at all. He rolled up his pants cuffs and the sleeves of his shirt and jacket, and then stepped out from behind the curtain.

"You look just like a real magician!" said Annie.

"Of course," said Jack, looking in the mirror and straightening his bow tie, "for that is exactly who I am. And so are you." He looked around the room. In the corner was a table on a pedestal. The top was covered with black velvet trimmed with gold fringe.

"Now let us prepare for our show. First we'll put the rabbits and doves in the hidden compartments of that table," he said.

"Yep," said Annie. "No problem."

Jack and Annie began preparing their props quietly and expertly, as if they'd done it a thousand times before. Jack picked up the rabbit cage and set it on the table. He pressed a small trapdoor in the middle of the velvet-covered tabletop, and the door flapped down.

"Here you go, bunnies," said Jack. He lifted the three small rabbits out of their cage and placed them comfortably in one of the table's hidden compartments. "See you soon."

While Jack took care of the rabbits, Annie handled the birds. She opened a second small door on the tabletop and carefully placed the two white doves into another secret compartment. "They look happy in there," she said.

Jack set the deck of cards in the center of the table. Annie hid the two wands inside the sleeves of her tuxedo jacket.

Jack pulled his pocket watch from his pants. "Eight-fifteen," he said.

Annie smiled. "We have fifty minutes of magic left," she said.

Jack slipped the watch into the pocket of his tuxedo jacket. Annie arranged the silver rings on top of the table.

A knock came at the door and Mr. Wilson looked into the room.

"Ready? Jolly Jack? Amazing Annie?" the stage manager asked.

This time, the roar of the crowd did not alarm Jack in the least. In fact, it thrilled him. "Yes, indeed, Mr. Wilson! Thank you!" he said with a jolly laugh.

"If you'd be so kind, Mr. Wilson, please set our table center stage," said Annie.

"Hank! Butch!" Mr. Wilson shouted. Two stage-hands immediately appeared. They picked up the table and carried it out of the dressing room. When the stage crew was gone, Jack and Annie pulled on their white gloves.

"You sure you feel okay about doing this?" Annie asked.

"Totally." Jack smiled at her. He tightened his gloves and wiggled his fingers. Then he put on his top hat. "Let's go, my dear," he said, leading the way out the door. "It's showtime!"

CHAPTER SIX

Jolly Jack and the Amazing Annie

As the orchestra played, Mr. Wilson guided Jack and Annie through the backstage area. "Watch out, kids," he said. "Like I said before, it's a tough crowd out there tonight."

Jack smiled confidently. *No crowd is too tough for us,* he thought.

Hank and Butch set the table with Jack and Annie's props center stage behind the closed curtain. The stage was lit with a soft rosy light.

"Places!" called Mr. Wilson.

Jack and Annie nodded and calmly took their

places in front of the table. They heard a long drumroll, then a cymbal crash. They heard Mr. Dewey speaking to the audience from in front of the curtain:

"Ladies and gentlemen! Welcome to the Great Houdini show! I have a very special and wonderful surprise for you this evening. As you may know, the Bambini Brothers were scheduled to be our opening act. But instead, it will be your great good fortune to welcome a truly remarkable pair of young illusionists. These master magicians have performed in theaters all around the world, and tonight they are here to perform for *you*! Ladies and gentlemen, I give you Jolly Jack and the Amazing Annie!"

A trumpet blasted, the curtain rose, and the crowd clapped and whistled as Jack and Annie stepped into a yellow spotlight.

Looking out at the audience, Jack chuckled like a seasoned performer. His heart pounded, but not with fear. It pounded with an excitement that made him want to do his best.

"Good evening, friends!" Jack shouted over the applause. "They call me Jolly Jack because nothing brings me greater joy than entertaining folks like *you*! And they call my sister Amazing Annie because—" Jack held his gloved hand out toward Annie.

"I love to amaze you with my amazing ability to amaze you!" Annie shouted.

The cymbals crashed. The crowd laughed.

"Do not let our youthful appearance fool you!" Annie went on. "My brother and I have traveled the globe to discover mysteries both ancient and modern!"

Jack took off his top hat and turned it toward the crowd. "I direct your attention to my hat," he said. "As you can see, the inside is quite ordinary. But strange things happen with this hat, especially when I touch it with a wand given to us by an Arabian princess."

Jack looked around. "Oh, dear, I seem to have forgotten my wand."

Annie stepped forward. She swept her right

arm in front of her—and *presto!* A wand appeared in her hand! Jack knew that when she waved her arm, she had simply allowed one of the hidden wands to slip from her sleeve.

The cymbals crashed.

The crowd cheered.

Annie grinned triumphantly and bowed.

While Annie was distracting everyone, Jack casually put his hat upside down on the velvet tabletop, over one of the hidden trapdoors. As he set the hat down, he pressed on the trapdoor and it flapped open.

"Thank you, Amazing Annie!" Jack called.

Annie handed Jack the wand, and he stepped back and waved it around the brim of the top hat.

The crowd grew quiet.

In a deep, mysterious voice, Jack intoned, "*Zoom-bally-win-doo-chee-gone-hay!* Which means, *Oh, marvelous hat, what do you have for me today?*"

Jack tapped the hat, stepped back from the table, and turned to Annie. "My dear, may I ask you to check my hat, please?" he said. "I have a feeling it holds a surprise."

There was a drumroll as Annie slowly reached into the hat. Jack knew she was pushing down on the top of the hat, which also had a secret flap.

A small white rabbit suddenly leapt from the secret compartment, through the hat, and into Annie's arms!

The orchestra played triumphant music, and the audience cheered.

Two more rabbits jumped out! Each time, Annie caught the rabbits and pretended to be surprised.

The cymbals crashed.

The audience laughed and clapped.

Annie handed the rabbits to Hank and Butch,

who carried them offstage. Then she took off her own hat. "Ladies and gentlemen!" she shouted. "As you can see, my hat is as empty as my brother's was." She showed the inside of the hat to the audience. "But it also holds wonders."

Annie set her hat on the table beside Jack's, carefully placing it on top of the second hidden door. "Oh, I'm going to need another wand!" she said. This time, she swept her left arm in front of her, and *presto!* The second wand appeared in her hand.

As the crowd applauded, Annie waved the wand over her hat. In a strange voice, she said, "*Zoom-bally-hula-hula-hi-ho-hay!* Which means, *Oh, wondrous hat, send new friends our way!*"

Jack reached into the hat, pushed down on the secret flap, then gently lifted out a dove. As the crowd cheered and clapped, he reached in again and took out the second dove. Jack handed the birds to Annie. They perched on her fingers as she lifted her hands into the air. The birds flapped their wings, bowing to the audience.

The cymbals crashed.

The crowd cheered and clapped.

While Annie distracted the crowd with the birds, Jack scooped the deck of cards off the table and stepped into the shadows. Behind his back, he divided the deck equally. Then he hid the two halves in the palms of his hands.

Annie gave the doves to Hank and Butch. Then she turned back to the crowd. "I believe my brother has something to share with you now!" Annie shouted. "Jolly Jack?"

Jack took Annie's place in the spotlight. "Are there any cardplayers in the house?" he called.

Many in the audience raised their hands. Some laughed loudly and teased each other.

"Well then, my friends," said Jack, "my strong advice to you tonight is *never* play cards with a magician!" As he spoke, he secretly gripped the edge of the card stack in his right hand. Using his thumb, he expertly inched the top card up until it was just behind his fingers.

All the while, Jack kept talking: "But oddly, some folks are foolish enough to challenge me to a game. Therefore, I never travel anywhere without a deck, but I prefer my cards to remain invisible until I am ready to use them!"

Jack then raised his right hand and flipped out the card, pretending to pluck it out of the air. The audience gasped. Cymbals clashed.

"Of course, you can't play a card game with only one card!" Jack said. He reached into the air with his left hand. "Ah, good! Here is another . . . and another . . . and another!"

The drummer pounded his drums each time Jack appeared to snatch a card from the air. He produced card after card. "What's this? Another! Another!" Finally, he said, "My goodness! I seem to have gathered an entire deck. Who wants to play a game?"

The cymbals crashed. The crowd cheered and Jack bowed.

Annie stepped into the spotlight, holding up three large rings. "Once upon a time, in a palace in China, we learned the ancient art of magic rings," she said.

Jack knew that one of the rings had a tiny opening in it. Annie hid the opening between her thumb and index finger so no one could see it.

"These are three solid rings," Annie told the crowd. "There is no way on earth to link them together!" She banged the rings against one another, making a show of trying to fit them together. Each time she failed.

Jack stepped forward. "But deep in the palace of the emperor," he said, "a Chinese sage taught us a magical song." Jack waved his wand over the first ring and sang, *"Hong-hong-hong-hong!"*

Annie banged the rings together again. This time she slipped the solid rings through the hidden opening in the other ring. Her hands moved so swiftly no one could see what she was doing.

"Once again, the magic song has worked!" she shouted, holding up the three connected rings.

Cymbals crashed.

As the crowd applauded, Annie easily disconnected the rings. Then she tossed the two solid ones high into the air. When they came down,

she caught them so they slipped perfectly through the tiny opening of the third ring.

Annie held up the connected rings, and the orchestra played triumphant music. As she bowed, the audience clapped and cheered wildly.

Jack joined her in the spotlight. "You have been most agreeable and welcoming tonight!" he shouted. "We will think of you fondly for years to come. But now we must leave you. During intermission, you can prepare your minds and nerves, in anticipation of the *most* amazing escape artist of all time: the *Great Houdini!*"

Trumpets sounded. Everyone cheered and stamped their feet.

Jack and Annie each bowed with a flourish. They raised their top hats to the crowd. Then, laughing and waving, they ran offstage, and the curtain came down.

CHAPTER SEVEN

Hurry Up, Houdini!

"Well, my dear," said Annie, "we did it!"

"We were brilliant!" said Jack.

Smiling, they pulled off their white gloves and grabbed their top hats. Hank and Butch quickly appeared and carried away their table and props. "Good show! Good show!" they said.

"Thanks, guys," said Jack, pulling off his bow tie.

"What time is it?" Annie asked.

Jack pulled out his pocket watch. "Eight-forty-eight," he said. "Our timing was perfect. We even have seventeen minutes of magic left over!"

"And Houdini should be in his dressing room now, since he goes on at nine," said Annie. "While we're still great magicians, should we try to talk to him? Maybe even show him a trick or two?"

"Yes!" said Jack.

Jack and Annie hurried off the stage. When they reached the dressing rooms, they found Mr. Dewey outside Houdini's door. He was pacing up and down, wringing his hands. "He's not *here*!" he cried. "He's not *here*!"

"Who?" said Jack.

"Houdini?" said Annie.

"Who else?" shouted Mr. Dewey. "He's not here! N-O-T! H-E-R-E!"

"Where is he? What happened to him?" asked Jack.

"Who knows?" cried Mr. Dewey. "All I know is that this is a disaster! The hooligans will demand their money back! And probably tear the theater apart! I'm facing ruin! Disgrace! All is lost!"

The stage door banged open, and Mr. Wilson

rushed in. "No sign of him outside, Boss," he said.

"Ohhh, Wilson!" cried Mr. Dewey. "We're doomed! We're doomed!"

Mr. Wilson nodded grimly.

Jack looked at his pocket watch. "Ten to nine," he said. "He could still make it in time."

Mr. Dewey raised his arms in the air, as if calling out to Houdini wherever he was. "Hurry up, Houdini! Hurry up!" he cried. Then he buried his head in his hands.

Oh, brother, thought Jack. Mr. Dewey was nuts. But where *was* Houdini? He and Annie needed him, too—or they'd never learn a secret of greatness from him.

"Listen, kids, if he's not here by nine, you'll have to go back out," Mr. Wilson said to Jack and Annie.

"Back out where?" said Jack.

"Onstage," said Mr. Wilson.

Mr. Dewey looked up. "Yes!" he cried. "You said you knew hundreds of tricks! Just keep performing till he shows up—*if* he shows up! Hold the crowd till he comes. Hold 'em if he doesn't come! Save me! I'll pay you!"

"No, no, you don't have to do that," said Annie. "We're happy to help."

"Annie, stop!" Jack whispered. "Our magic hour's almost up." He looked back at the theater owner. "I'm sorry, but I'm afraid we can't go back out there."

"You must! You must!" said Mr. Dewey. "They love you! Go out and save my theater! Save my life! Please!"

"Whoa, take it easy," Jack said, trying to calm the hysterical man. He didn't know what else to say.

"Don't worry, Mr. Dewey, we'll help," said Annie.

"Thank you!" cried Mr. Dewey. "I'll look for Houdini outside!"

Mr. Dewey hurried away. Mr. Wilson called to his crew and told them to put the rabbits and birds back in the hidden compartments of the table.

"Let's talk," Jack said to Annie. They slipped

into their dressing room, and Jack closed the door.

"I know you said yes only because Mr. Dewey was losing his mind," said Jack. "But I don't see how we can do this."

"Well, if we go on at nine, we'll have five good minutes," said Annie.

"I know, but what if Houdini's still not here after five good minutes?" said Jack.

"Maybe we could hold their attention some other way," said Annie. "We could at least try."

"Hmm." Jack thought for a moment. "Actually, maybe we can get away with doing the same tricks we did before," he said. "Now that we know how they work, they shouldn't be that hard. We know how to push on the tops of the hats. We know about the hidden compartments in the table. We know about the opening in the ring."

"Yeah . . . right. Right, easy," said Annie. "You can keep doing card tricks, and I can keep throwing the rings around."

Mr. Wilson opened the door, and sounds from the audience filled the room. Jack could hear feet stamping and people chanting, "Hoo-dee-nee! Hoo-dee-nee!"

"Everything's back onstage," said Mr. Wilson. "Ready to tame the lions?"

Jack still felt the confidence that came from being a great magician. "Showtime!" he said.

"No problem!" said Annie.

Jack and Annie left the dressing room and followed Mr. Wilson through the backstage area.

"Dewey's out on the avenue, looking for Houdini," said Mr. Wilson. "Take your places, and I'll pull the curtain."

Jack and Annie strode onto the stage and stood in front of the table. Jack looked at his pocket watch. It was nine o'clock.

The curtain rose to great fanfare. The audience clapped and cheered. It took a moment for everyone to realize they were looking at Jack and Annie again. After a stunned silence, some people started booing and hissing.

Jack stepped forward. He tipped his hat and laughed his jolly laugh. "What a terrible surprise, eh?" he shouted. "You didn't know Jolly Jack is the secret identity of the Great Houdini, did you?"

More booing and hissing.

"Seriously, folks, I understand your disappointment," said Jack. "But the world's greatest magician is preparing himself backstage right now to give you the best show you've ever seen. So please allow Jolly Jack and the Amazing Annie to entertain you for a few more minutes!"

The audience quieted down, but then someone yelled, "We want Houdini!"

"Take it outside, pal!" said Jack. "So do we!"

The audience laughed.

Jack turned to Annie. "The wand, sister dear."

Annie expertly dropped the wand down her sleeve into her hand. The cymbals crashed. But this time, there wasn't much applause.

Annie gave the wand to Jack. As he placed his hat over the hidden compartment on the table, he secretly pushed down on the trapdoor. Jack then waved the wand around the brim of the hat. He opened his mouth to speak—but suddenly, *horribly,* he couldn't think of anything to say!

Holding the wand in midair, Jack turned to Annie. She looked confused, too. Their hour of being great stage magicians had ended. The magic was over.

Some people yelled from the audience. Jack felt embarrassed and self-conscious. He couldn't believe he was trying to perform magic in front of a gazillion people. It was like a nightmare! He couldn't move or speak!

Annie rushed over. She reached into Jack's hat and pushed down on the top. Out jumped the rabbits—one, two, three! But this time, Annie couldn't catch them, and they jumped to the floor and hopped around the stage.

The audience laughed and booed.

Annie put her hat over the second trapdoor and pushed down on the top. Out flew the birds. They circled above the table while Annie grinned foolishly. "See? Magic doves . . . again," she said. The stagehands came out and tried to gather up all the creatures.

The audience booed.

The musicians didn't know what to do. They played random violin squeaks, drum sounds, and trumpet wails.

Jack grabbed the deck of cards. "Um . . . are there still some cardplayers here?" he said. He thrust out his arm. Instead of a card appearing in his hand, the whole deck flew into the air.

BLAAAAH! played the trombone.

Annie grabbed the three silver rings, but she fumbled them, too, and they clattered to the floor.

Again, the trombone played, *BLAAAAH!*

The audience laughter and booing had turned to shouting, "Hoo-dee-nee! Hoo-dee-nee!" People stamped their feet.

Mr. Wilson yelled from the wings, "Different tricks, kids! Do something new!"

Jack was desperate to leave the stage. He grabbed Annie by the arm. "Let's get out of here!" he said.

"Wait," she said, squinting out at the crowd. "Listen."

Jack heard people yelling, "Hurrah!" Then he heard cheers and clapping!

Has Houdini arrived? Jack wondered.

The audience clapped and chanted louder than ever: "Hoo-dee-nee! Hoo-dee-nee!"

Mr. Dewey was leading a man and woman down the aisle, toward the stage. The woman's hat was piled high with bananas and roses. "Is that Bess?" said Jack.

"Yes," said Annie. "It's Bess and Harry!"

"How weird! What are they doing?" said Jack. "Are they coming to help us?"

Mr. Dewey led Bess and Harry onto the stage.

Bess rushed over to Jack and Annie. "What are you two doing here?" she said to them.

"What are *you* two doing here?" said Annie.

"We got trapped on the Trip to the Moon! The gears got stuck!" said Bess. "So you kids are performers?"

"We were just filling in for the Bambini Brothers!" said Jack. "And then—"

"Hey—what's Harry doing?" said Annie.

Harry had walked down to the footlights. He was bowing to the crowd! And the audience was screaming and cheering.

Harry raised his hands to quiet them. Then he motioned to Jack and Annie. "Come here, kiddos!" he said.

Jack and Annie walked downstage. Harry put one arm around Jack's shoulders and the other around Annie's.

Then he looked back out at the crowd. "Folks, wasn't that the worst magic act you've ever seen? Ha! It's all part of the show! I asked my young friends to warm you up for me . . . and that they did! Now I think you're ready, no?"

"Yes!" the audience screamed. "Yes!"

Harry looked from Annie to Jack. "You can relax now, kiddos," he said. "The Great Houdini has arrived."

CHAPTER EIGHT

Master of Escape

"You ... you?" breathed Annie.

"You're the Great Houdini?" said Jack. He couldn't believe it!

"Just give us a moment to set up our show!" Houdini shouted to the audience. "Sit tight, and we'll be back quick as a wink! In the meantime, how about a nice hand for these funny little magicians?"

Music played, Jack and Annie bowed, the crowd roared enthusiastically, and the red curtain came down. Bess rushed over to Jack and Annie.

"Thanks for helping us out!" she said.

"We had no idea you had a comedy act," Harry said.

"We had no idea you were the Great Houdini!" said Annie.

"That's what we figured," said Bess. "Forgive us for having a little fun with you two."

"Harry! Hurry!" Mr. Dewey said. The theater owner led Houdini back to his dressing room.

"Thanks again, you crazy kids, for covering for us!" said Bess, hugging Jack and Annie.

"Everyone, please clear the stage!" Mr. Wilson said. "We have to reset!"

"Stick around and watch us!" Bess said to Jack and Annie. She guided them to a couple of chairs just offstage. "Sit here! I have to help Harry." She hurried back to the dressing room.

As crowd noises filled the theater, Annie turned to Jack. "Can you believe it?" she said.

"No . . . I can't—I can't believe it . . . ," said Jack. He was in a daze.

"Maybe we'll learn the secret of greatness

from him now," said Annie hopefully.

"Oh, right," said Jack. He pulled off his gloves and looked at the Ring of Truth on his finger. He hoped it would soon start to glow.

While the Houdinis prepared for the show, the stagehands found all the rabbits and doves and put them back in their cages. They picked up the cards and rings and hauled the table away.

"Set Harry's cabinet center stage!" Mr. Wilson called.

Hank and Butch carried a wooden cabinet onto the stage. Black fabric covered three sides of it, and a black curtain hung in front.

Just as the audience began to stamp their feet, Mr. Dewey led the Houdinis out of their dressing room. Bess was wearing white tights and a short pleated dress. Her delicate face was framed by a ring of dark curls. Harry was dressed in an elegant black suit, his hair combed back neatly.

The curtain rose, and the orchestra played a rousing tune.

Bess stood beside the cabinet while Harry

stepped into a spotlight. For a long moment, he gazed intensely at the audience. When the noisy crowd grew quiet, he spoke in a voice that carried all the way to the back of the theater.

"Ladies and gentlemen, I, Harry Houdini, would like to make a bet with you! I'll bet a thousand dollars there is no lock that can hold me captive tonight! They don't call me the Master of Escape for nothing!"

From that moment on, Harry Houdini *was* the Master of Escape. As the orchestra played, he performed easily, with humor and confidence. Several times during his act, he invited volunteers onstage to make sure all his locks were securely locked and all his knots were tightly tied.

During his first trick, Houdini asked the audience volunteers to check three pairs of handcuffs that Bess had locked around his wrists. Then he stepped inside his cabinet.

Bess closed the black curtain. "Let's count to ten together!" she called to the crowd.

Everyone counted: "One! Two! Three! . . ."

On the count of ten, Houdini threw open the curtain—his handcuffs dangling from his hand!

Jack and Annie gasped. "How did he do that?" Jack said.

Harry did the trick again with a new level of difficulty. This time, Bess not only locked handcuffs around Houdini's wrists, she also wrapped chains around his ankles and secured them with padlocks. Again, excited volunteers made certain that all the locks were truly locked.

When the black curtain closed, Bess asked everyone to count again. On the count of ten, Harry threw open the curtain—freed from his shackles and handcuffs. The crowd clapped and cheered.

"And now," he said, "the Master of Escape will share with you his most thrilling and dangerous escape to date!"

Houdini dashed offstage. The orchestra played scary-sounding music as Hank and Butch brought out a huge milk can and placed it inside the cabinet. Audience members whispered to each other as the stagehands filled the giant can with buckets of water.

Harry then reappeared dressed in an oldfashioned black bathing suit. Bess put the three pairs of handcuffs around his wrists again. After volunteers checked the locks, Houdini climbed inside the milk can.

Jack and Annie stood up to watch.

Houdini lowered himself into the water until he was completely inside the can. Water splashed over the sides. Bess then closed the lid, padlocked it, and pulled the black curtain.

While the can was out of sight, the orchestra played *tick-tock, tick-tock.* Jack could hardly breathe as one minute went by . . . two minutes . . . Someone in the audience cried out with alarm.

How does Harry keep from drowning? Jack wondered anxiously. *How can he undo handcuffs in such a tight space?*

Suddenly Houdini threw back the curtain. He was standing in front of the milk can, dripping wet! He had escaped again! He stepped to the side and

pointed to the lid of the can—it was still locked firmly in place!

Bess brought Harry a red robe, and the audience cheered. The orchestra played triumphant music.

The whole time Houdini had been performing his tricks, Jack had listened carefully to everything he'd said:

"Ladies and gentlemen, my brain is the key that sets me free!"

"Ladies and gentlemen, my chief task is to conquer fear!"

"Ladies and gentlemen, an old trick in a new dress is always a pleasant change!"

Every time Houdini said something that sounded meaningful, Jack checked the Ring of Truth. He kept hoping that some secret of greatness would be revealed. But no matter what Harry said, the gold ring didn't glow.

After the milk can trick, the stage crew replaced the can with a steamer trunk.

"Finally, for old times' sake, I close with the act that first made me famous," said Houdini.

The drummer played a drumroll. Then Houdini shouted: "The world-famous original Metamorphosis in three seconds! For this amazing feat, I will share the spotlight with the one and only *Mrs.* Houdini!"

Harry took Bess's hand, and she curtsied for the crowd.

"Years ago, I met this beautiful gal right here on Coney Island," Houdini said. "I love her with all my heart. But now she must become my prisoner."

The audience laughed as a stagehand brought out a short, thick rope. Harry quickly tied Bess's hands behind her back. "Dear one, I must now ask you to step into this bag." Bess stepped into a large canvas bag, and Houdini tied the bag at the top.

With Hank and Butch's help, Houdini lifted Bess into the steamer trunk that had been placed inside the cabinet. Then Hank and Butch closed the trunk, wrapped it with a rope, and locked it with padlocks. After volunteers checked to see that the trunk was securely bound and locked, Houdini shouted, "Behold a miracle!"

Remaining inside the cabinet with the trunk,

Harry closed the black curtain. As the audience watched and waited, three loud claps rang out from behind the curtain.

The curtain was thrown open. Bess stood in front of the roped and locked trunk, completely free! She quickly cut the rope around the trunk, unlocked the padlocks, untied the sack—and out jumped the Great Houdini!

Everyone leapt to their feet, applauding and roaring, "Bravo! Bravo!"

Jack and Annie clapped and shouted with them as the Houdinis bowed again and again.

"Ladies and gentlemen, let me assure you that I have shown you no supernatural powers tonight!" Harry shouted. "Please know that magic is all tricks! Everything you saw tonight was illusion!"

And Harry Houdini is the greatest Master of Illusion in the world, Jack thought.

Jack's only disappointment was that all during the Great Houdini show, the Ring of Truth had not glowed once. Not even the tiniest bit.

CHAPTER NINE

The Real Story

After the curtain closed, Jack could hear the joyful crowd leaving the theater. Mr. Dewey, Mr. Wilson, Butch, and Hank rushed from the wings to congratulate the Houdinis.

Mr. Dewey actually went down on his knees to thank them. "You have made my audience very happy!" he exclaimed. "And when my audience is happy, I am happy, too! Great show! Great show!"

"Man, he's *really* lost it," Jack said.

Annie laughed. "Come on, I want to tell them 'Great show,' too," she said.

But as Jack and Annie started toward the Houdinis, some teenage boys rushed onstage ahead of them.

"Sorry, boys," said Mr. Wilson, stepping between the boys and the Houdinis. "Mr. Houdini is exhausted from his magnificent performance. You'll have to buy a ticket and come back again!"

"Come on, Harry, let's get you two out of here!" Mr. Dewey said.

As Mr. Dewey whisked Harry and Bess backstage, Jack and Annie followed them. Mr. Dewey ushered the couple into their dressing room. He hurried in after them and closed the door.

Annie was about to knock, but Jack stopped her. "Don't bother them yet," he said. "Let them relax a minute first. We'll see them when they come out."

"Good idea," said Annie.

Jack and Annie waited outside the Houdinis' dressing room door as the crew cleared all the hooligan fans off the stage.

They waited as Hank and Butch took away

Houdini's cabinet, his milk can, and his steamer trunk. They waited as Mrs. Crenshaw collected the bird and rabbit cages and carried them away. They waited as Mr. Wilson swept the floor and turned off the stage lights.

"They should be relaxed by now," said Annie.

"No kidding," said Jack. He tapped softly on the door. There was no answer.

Annie knocked louder. "Bess? Harry?" she called.

Still, no one answered. Annie tried the handle, but the door was locked.

"They're gone," said Mr. Wilson, passing by Jack and Annie in the hall.

"Gone?" said Annie.

"Yes, both the Houdinis left a while ago," the stage manager said.

"Left? How?" asked Jack. He and Annie had been watching the door every minute!

"Mr. Dewey took them through the secret exit out of the stars' dressing room," said Mr. Wilson. "It goes through the basement and out of the theater. Otherwise, they'd be mobbed by all the crazy fans."

"So they're really gone?" said Jack.

"They don't call Harry the Master of Escape for nothing," Mr. Wilson said. "You'd better change out of your costumes and get going, too. We'll be locking up the building soon."

Jack and Annie walked down the hall and into their dressing room. "I can't believe it!" Annie wailed. "We didn't even get to tell them 'Great show.'"

"Worse than that, we didn't get to find out a secret of greatness," said Jack. He held up his finger with the Ring of Truth. "The ring didn't glow all night."

"Well, I guess all we can do is get dressed and go look for them," said Annie.

Jack and Annie quickly changed out of the tuxedos and back into their street clothes. Jack grabbed his bag and put his watch in the pocket of his pants.

"Come on, hurry!" said Annie. She and Jack

rushed out the back door of the theater. They ran down the dark alley, past the row of garbage cans, and out to the street.

Surf Avenue was still bright with lights and just as busy as before. The sidewalks were still crowded with lots of people. The old-timey cars and horses and buggies filled the cobbled street.

"They could be anywhere," said Jack. "They could even have gone home."

"Let's try Luna Park," said Annie.

"Why would they go back there?" asked Jack. "Especially after getting trapped on their Trip to the Moon?"

"I don't know. There's lots they might want to do there," said Annie. She gasped.

"Ice cream!" Jack and Annie said together. At the same moment, they'd each remembered Bess saying *"Ice cream always comes after the show."*

"To the ice cream stand!" said Annie.

"And fast!" said Jack.

Jack and Annie took off up the street, dodging people along the way. They ran to the tall arches,

where ticket sellers in chariots were still welcoming people into Luna Park.

"Admission, ten cents each," one said.

Jack and Annie dumped the rest of their pennies into the ticket seller's hands. Then they took off, dashing up the broad avenue, weaving around couples and children and barkers on stilts and unicycles.

When they came to the ice cream stand, they found a line of people waiting to buy cones. Panting, Jack looked up and down the line.

The two Houdinis were nowhere to be seen.

Jack's spirits fell. But Annie poked him. "What?" Jack said.

Annie pointed at the terrace.

Jack looked up. Harry and Bess were sitting on a bench side by side, holding ice cream cones. Their big hats hid their faces.

Jack laughed. "Now I get it! They wear those hats so fans won't recognize them," he said.

"Well, they can't fool us," said Annie. "C'mon."

Annie and Jack headed over to the bench.

When they were close, Annie put her finger to her lips. Jack understood what she meant. Without greeting Harry or Bess, Jack and Annie sat down next to them.

"Great ice cream, huh?" said Annie.

"Great," said Bess, not looking up.

"Would you call it the *greatest in the world*?" asked Jack.

Tilting her head, Bess peeked out from under the brim of her hat. She laughed loudly. "Hey, Harry! Look!" she exclaimed. "It's our little friends!"

Harry raised his hat, then laughed too. "The crazy kiddos!" he said. "So what's the story? What the heck were you two doing up on that stage tonight?"

"We just love to perform," said Annie with a giggle.

"We just love to make fools of ourselves," said Jack.

"Making a fool of yourself is a brave thing to do," Harry said, smiling.

"That's what Aristotle once told us," said Annie, "more or less."

Jack glanced at the Ring of Truth. It wasn't glowing.

"Mr. Houdini!" someone said. A man stood in front of the bench. He started to clap.

"Oh, dear," murmured Bess.

"You were unbelievable tonight!" the man said. "I never saw anything like what you did!"

Other people turned to look. They recognized Harry, too, and began gathering in front of the bench, telling him how great he was. Harry finished his ice cream cone. Then he stood up and started shaking hands with his admirers.

Bess shook her head and sighed. "He's always nice to people," she said to Jack and Annie. "No matter how tired he is."

Harry's fans kept asking questions: "How do you do it?" "How did you escape from those handcuffs?" "How'd you get out of that milk can?"

"First of all, let me assure you again that I have no supernatural powers," said Harry. "It's all illusion. These skills just happen to come easily to me. Always have. I remember when I was a kid . . ."

Jack looked at the Ring of Truth. Nothing.

"That's not the *real* story," Bess said quietly to Jack and Annie, her eyes twinkling.

"What *is* the real story?" Annie asked her.

"Harry's always worked very, very hard," she said. "He's worked all his life. When he was a little boy, he sold newspapers and flowers. He performed in a neighborhood children's circus. A few years later, he hopped trains and tried to get work in Milwaukee, Kansas City, New York. He practiced coin tricks and card tricks for hours every day. He read every book he could find on magic. He practiced and practiced and practiced. Those skills did *not* come naturally to him. They came from hard work and more practice than most people could endure."

Jack thought about how he and Annie had only done their magic tricks *once*, with the help of the magic mist. No wonder they'd failed so spectacularly the second time.

"So his secret is *hard work*?" said Annie.

"You've got it, kiddo," said Bess. "But that's not such a big secret, is it? Anyone would have to work hard to be truly great at something."

"Yeah, they would," said Jack.

"Oh, wow," Annie whispered to Jack. She pointed at his hand.

Jack looked down and smiled. The Ring of Truth was finally glowing.

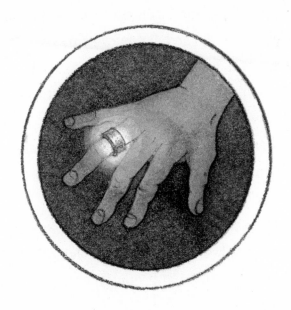

CHAPTER TEN

Best Escape Act Ever

Annie grinned at Jack. "Done!" she whispered.

"Done!" Jack agreed. "Now we can leave."

"Harry and I have to go, too," said Bess. "I want to get him out of here before he attracts the wrong types."

"Hooligans and crazy fans?" asked Annie.

"You got it," said Bess. "Harry!" she called. "Time's up!"

Harry excused himself from the crowd of people and walked back to the bench. "Thanks, sweetheart," he said. "I couldn't escape." He winked at Bess, then looked at Jack and Annie. "They think I do truly magical things. But it's not true. It's all just entertainment. It's all tricks."

"Harry's never seen anyone do a trick he couldn't do himself," said Bess.

"That's a fact," said Harry. "Nothing. Ever."

"Amazing," said Annie.

"Amazing, yes, but it's also a great sadness," said Harry, frowning. "The world's lost its wonder for me. I would be so happy just *once* to see a bit of magic I could never do or never explain."

"Really?" said Jack.

"Yes, but it's not going to happen," Harry said with a sigh. "Well, I'm ready, my love. Let's go home."

"Yes, let's," said Bess, standing. She looked at Jack and Annie. "Which way are you two going?"

"Just down that way," Jack said. And then he had a great idea. He smiled at Annie. "Let's walk them as far as the Japanese Tea Garden."

Annie's eyes lit up. She seemed to know what Jack was thinking. "Good plan!" she said.

"Sure, let's all go together," said Bess.

Harry, Bess, Jack, and Annie all stepped down from the terrace and started up the broad avenue. The band was playing "After the Ball Is Over." The crowd had thinned out. The lights were starting to dim.

"What a fantastic park," said Harry. "Did you try many rides? The pirate ship? Or the navy ship sailing the deep ocean? The Arctic trip?"

"No, but we've done all those things before," said Jack.

"Did you get to experience the cyclone attraction, too?" said Bess. "The volcano? The big fire?"

"Actually we've experienced all *those* things, too," said Jack.

"Really?" said Bess. "So you must have been in this park a long time?"

"No, I was talking about real life," Jack said matter-of-factly. "My sister and I travel in a magic tree house to different times and places and have lots of adventures."

Annie grinned. "Jack's telling the truth," she

said. "We've been all through time."

Harry and Bess chuckled. "Sounds like a good act," said Harry.

"It does, doesn't it?" said Bess delightedly. "Where else do you perform your act, besides Coney Island?"

"We don't really perform this act for anyone," said Annie. "It's usually a secret."

"But we'll show it to *you*," said Jack.

"Lucky us," said Bess, winking at Harry.

"The tree house is parked in the Japanese Tea Garden," said Annie. "You want to see it? It'll only take a minute."

"Sure, why not?" said Harry.

Bess and Harry followed Jack and Annie over to the wooden gate that led to the Japanese Tea Garden. They followed them through the gateway, up the pebble path, and over the small arched bridge to the cluster of trees.

"There," said Annie. She pointed up at one of the trees.

"A tree house! Well, how about that?" said

Harry. He sounded genuinely surprised. "I never
knew that was here." ·

"That's because it's only been here for a few
hours," said Annie.

"You want to watch us take off?" asked Jack.

"Take off?" said Bess.

"Yep, the tree house is going to take us back home to Pennsylvania now," said Jack, "to a time more than a hundred years from today."

"In the future," Annie added.

Bess and Harry laughed. "You two might be the looniest kids in the world," said Bess.

"Or the best actors!" said Harry.

"Wait and see . . . ," said Annie. She held out her hand. "Bye, Harry. It's been *great* knowing you."

Harry shook Annie's hand, and then he shook Jack's. Bess grabbed each of them and gave them big hugs. "You two kiddos are great!" she said, giggling. "You're just my kind of screwballs."

They all laughed. Then Jack and Annie climbed up the rope ladder. Inside the tree house, Annie picked up the Pennsylvania book, and she and Jack looked out the window. "Bye!" They both waved to Harry and Bess.

The Houdinis waved back.

"I wish we could go home," Annie whispered as she pointed to a picture of Frog Creek.

"Behold a miracle!" Jack shouted down to Bess

and Harry. He clapped three times. *One! Two! THREE!*

Then the wind started to blow.

The tree house started to spin.

It spun faster and faster.

Then everything was still.

Absolutely still.

$$\text{\textwon} \quad \text{\textwon} \quad \text{\textwon}$$

The Frog Creek woods were quiet and peaceful. The early-evening light filtered into the tree house. Jack and Annie were wearing their own clothes again.

"Now *that* was the best escape act ever," said Annie.

Jack smiled. "I wanted to make Harry happy. We showed him something he'll never be able to explain."

Jack looked at his watch. As always, no time had passed in Frog Creek while they'd been on their mission. "Six minutes to get home," said Jack.

"Yep, but first we have to write down our new secret of greatness," said Annie.

Jack pulled out a pencil and picked up the paper that was still lying on the floor. And under the word HUMILITY, he wrote:

HARD WORK

"Hard work," said Annie. "That's so simple."

"Yep," said Jack. "Sometimes the truth is amazingly simple." He placed the Ring of Truth on top of the paper. "And I'll leave this, too"—he took the little bottle from his backpack and placed it beside the ring—"for next time."

"Mist gathered at first light on the first day of the new moon on the Isle of Avalon," said Annie.

Jack closed his backpack. "Okay, that's it! Let's go! Mom's hot dogs are waiting!"

"Greatest in the world!" said Annie. The two of them climbed down from the ladder and headed through the trees.

"You know what?" said Annie.

"What?" asked Jack.

"You know how we were supposed to learn

a secret of greatness from the Great Houdini?" Annie said.

"Yep," said Jack.

"And we kept waiting for Harry to say or do something to make the ring glow?" said Annie.

"Yeah," said Jack.

"But in the end, we learned the secret from *Bess*, not Harry," said Annie.

"You're right," said Jack.

"So I think *Bess* was the Great Houdini that Merlin sent us to find," said Annie.

"Why do you think Bess was great?" asked Jack.

"Well, she was kind and funny and friendly," said Annie.

"Yeah . . . ," said Jack, "like you."

"Me?" said Annie. "Huh." She looked a little embarrassed. "Well, also she was a loyal person. She was loyal to Harry."

"That's true," said Jack.

"She was loyal like you are," said Annie.

"Me?" said Jack.

"Yep, you came right back when you realized I needed help," said Annie. "Even though I'd made you really mad."

"Well, you were loyal, too," said Jack. "You didn't hold a grudge because I'd left you."

"Me, loyal?" said Annie. "And kind and funny and friendly? You think I'm all that? Seriously? Me?"

"Okay, forget it," said Jack, grinning.

"No, I'm going to remember all those things," said Annie. "And the next time you're mad at me, I'm going to remind you how great I am. How loyal and kind and funny—"

"Okay, okay, that's enough!" said Jack. "Bye!" He took off running. He ran out of the Frog Creek woods, across the street, and down the sidewalk.

"Wait! Slow down! You can't escape from me!" called Annie. She ran after Jack as fast as she could and caught up with him before he reached home.

Author's Note

While doing my research for *Hurry Up, Houdini!*, I loved learning more about Beatrice "Bess" Houdini. Harry first met Bess in Coney Island in 1893 when he and his brother Dash were performing as a magic act called the Brothers Houdini, and eighteen-year-old Bess was singing and dancing with the Floral Sisters. Bess and Harry were married three weeks later. Bess became Harry's partner onstage as he continued to develop and perform his amazing illusions. For the next thirty years, the two traveled all over the world together.

I also had a great time learning more about Coney Island, New York. In its heyday in the early 1900s, Coney Island was famous for its spectacular amusement parks. The rides were unlike anything the world had ever seen. I decided to set this story in Luna Park and chose a combination of attractions from the first decade of the park's existence.

I think it would have been so exciting to have actually met the Houdinis and to have gone to Coney Island in the early 1900s. But the best thing about writing this book is that now I feel almost like I really did spend a summer evening in Luna Park with Bess and Harry long ago.

Turn the page for a sneak peek at *Magic Tricks from the Tree House!*

Where Did the Coin Go?

OBJECT: Trick your audience into thinking you've made a coin disappear.

What You Need:
- tinfoil
- four nickels
- scissors

PREPARATION: Tear off a piece of tinfoil that will be big enough to fold around a nickel. Rub the covered coin with your thumb so that you can see a clear outline and the details of the coin underneath. Be sure to do the edges, too.

Now carefully cut out around the coin you've made and *be sure* the sides show. Remove the real nickel. When you finish, the foil should look like a shiny coin.

1. Show that you've got five "nickels" in your hand. Keep the fake nickel slightly hidden by the real ones.

2. Close your hand into a fist. As you do so, crumple the tinfoil coin into a tiny ball with your thumb and push it under the other coins.

3. Open your hand. There are only four nickels. (The fake coin is a tiny ball hidden by the other nickels.)

Celebrate
Passport to Adventure
Reading Buddies Week
Coming October 12–19, 2013!

This week-long celebration in schools, libraries, bookstores, and homes encourages the model of "Buddy Reading." The Passport to Adventure program is designed to grow young people's literacy skills and to get books into the hands of all children.

Bring Magic Tree House to your school's stage!

Magic Tree House #1: *Dinosaurs Before Dark* is now a musical available for performance by young people!

Ask your teacher or director to contact Music Theatre International for more information:
BroadwayJr.com
Licensing@MTIshows.com
(212) 541-4684

Available now wherever books and ebooks are sold.

MagicTreeHouse.com
MTHClassroomAdventures.com

Coming in January 2014!

Jack and Annie are rescued by
Florence Nightingale after a scary accident!

Meet some of the greatest heroes of all time!

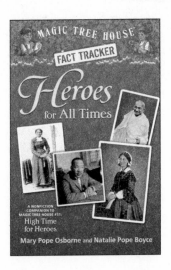